To Paulipops —remember to bend your knees!

First American edition published in 2007 by Carolrhoda Books, Inc.

Published in the United Kingdom by Templar Publishing,
an imprint of The Templar Company plc
Pippbrook Mill, London Road, Dorking, Surrey, RH4 1JE, UK

Copyright © 2007 by Shane McG

Carolrhoda Books, Inc.
A division of Lerner Publishing Group
241 First Avenue North
Minneapolis, MN 55401 U.S.A.

Website address: www.lernerbooks.com

Library of Congress Cataloging-in-Publication Data

McG, Shane.
Tennis, anyone? / by Shane McG. — 1st American ed.
p. cm.
Summary: When Tom receives a tennis racket for his seventh
birthday, he cannot figure out who to play with or what's fun about
it until his father helps him look at the sport in a new way.
ISBN-13: 978-0-8225-6901-5 (lib. bdg : alk. paper)
ISBN-10: 0-8225-6901-9 (lib. bdg. : alk. paper)
[1. Tennis—Fiction.]   I. Title.
PZ7.M47846213Te 2007
[E]—dc22   2006018746

Printed and bound in China
1 2 3 4 5 6 – CC – 12 11 10 09 08 07

"WHO PLAYS TENNIS?

Mom doesn't play tennis.

All she wants to do is stand on one leg humming and doing her yogurt."

"I think you mean yoga," Dad said.

Whatever.

It looks dumb.

"SO WHO PLAYS TENNIS?"

My cat, Smudgy, doesn't play tennis.

She spends her entire day **eating**...

and passing gas.

"PHEW! Smudgy!"

Tennis, Anyone?

Shane McG

Carolrhoda Books, Inc. Minneapolis • New York

Hi. I'm Tom Foley...

and I'm 7 years old.

I know this because yesterday was my birthday and I got lots of great presents.

They're amazing! They do lots of cool things, like BEEP and CRASH and WHIRR.

All except this one.

It doesn't DO anything.

Dad said it was a racket. You play tennis with it.

He said it's a lot of fun.

I wasn't convinced.

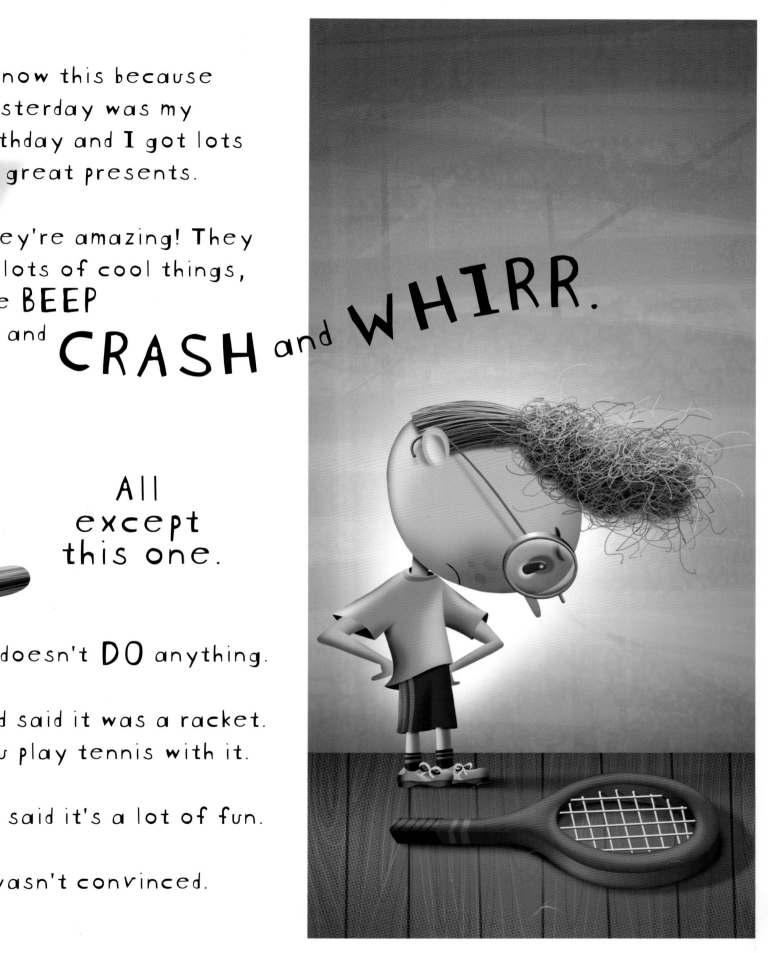

"WHO PLAYS TENNIS?"

I asked Dad.

My sister, Ida, doesn't play tennis.
In fact, she doesn't do **ANYTHING**.

(Except lie in her bedroom all day
talking to her friend Tania about
boys and shopping.)

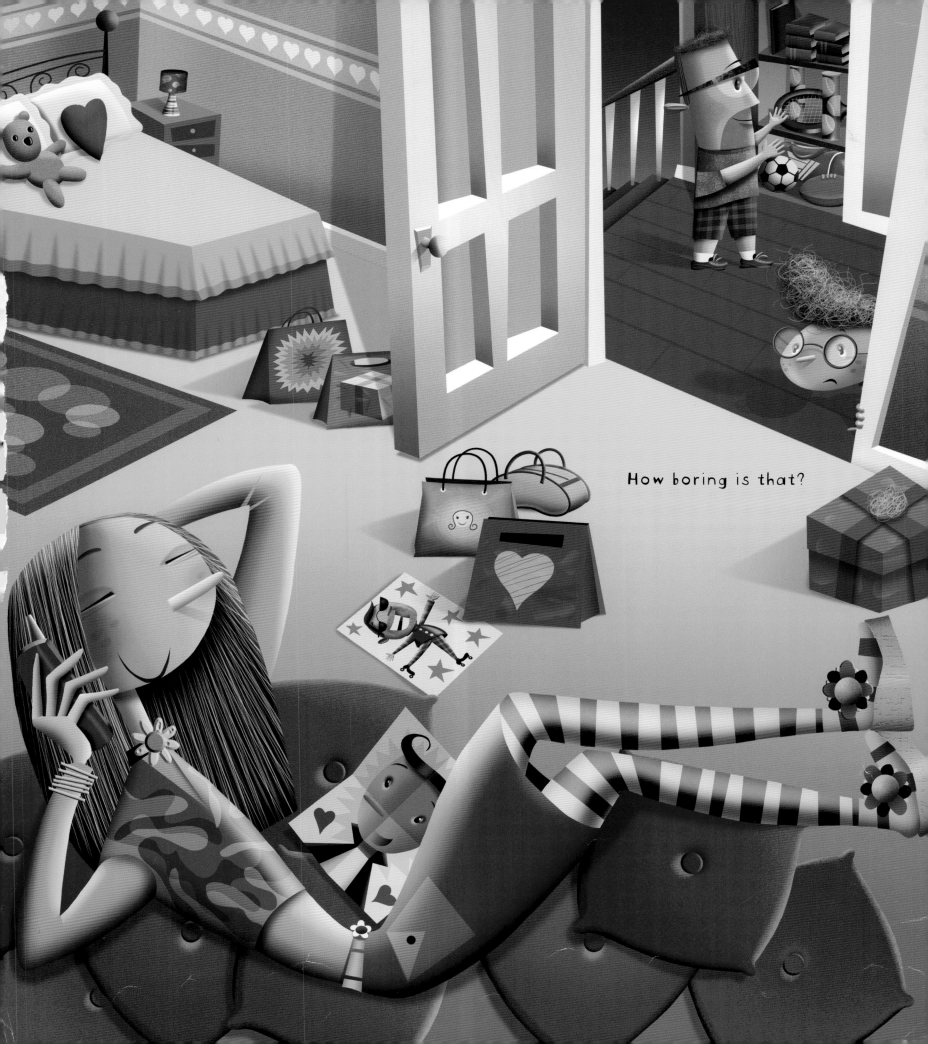

How boring is that?

My Best Friend, Kevin, doesn't play tennis either.

He spends all his time riding his cool new green bike.

Without giving me a turn.

EVER.

Actually, he's my Sixth-Best Friend.

And my dog, Spike, **definitely** doesn't play tennis.

He's way too busy chasing cars.

Poor ol' Spike. He never catches them.

My cuddly blue croc
certainly doesn't
play tennis.

That would be crazy!

He'd trip over the ball.

 I asked Dad one more time,

"WHO PLAYS TENNIS?

HELLO...?

DAD...?

WHERE ARE WE GOING?"

I don't think he was listening.

He was too

busy...

...hitting balls at me. I had to duck for cover.
I thought about running away, but I'm not a scaredy-cat.

"Don't worry," Dad said.

"When I hit the ball to you,
you hit it back to me.

Then I'll hit it back to you.

Then you hit it back to me.

Okay?"

"Okay."

I took a really **BIG** swing at the ball...

and fell over!

"You just need a little practice,"
said Dad.

...AND PRACTICE

is just what I did!

On the way home, Dad asked me,
"Who plays tennis, son?"

I said, "That's **easy-peasy**, Dad.

TOM FOLEY PLAYS TENNIS!"

My racket is **pretty cool** after all.

It doesn't beep or crash or whirr,
but you **CAN** play **TENNIS** with it...